WARM, DARK PLACES

WARM, DARK PLACES
H. L. GOLD

Kaplan tried to make a gesture of impatience. It was impossible because his arms were piled high with clothing. He followed his wife's pointing finger and succeeded in shrugging contemptuously.

Clad in pathetic rags, the hairiest, dirtiest tramp in the world stood outside the plate-glass window of Kaplan's dry-cleaning store and eagerly watched the stubby, garment-laden figure as it waddled toward the bandbox cleaning vat.

"Him?" Kaplan echoed sarcastically. "A bum like him is going to drive us out of business? Do you mind if I am asking you what with, Mrs. Genius?"

"Like my mother told me," Mrs. Kaplan retorted angrily, "a book you can't tell by its covers. So, rags he's wearing and he's dirty, that means he can't have money? You don't read in the papers, I suppose. Blind beggars don't own apartment houses and chauffeurs, I suppose, and people on relief don't ride cars down to get their checks. Besides, such a feeling I get when I look at him—like when a mouse looks at a cat."

"Pah!" Kaplan broke in good-humoredly. "Some foolishness."

"All right, Mr. Einstein, he's standing out there with a pencil and paper because somewhere else he ain't got to go."

"You think maybe you're wrong?" Kaplan almost snapped testily. "No. He's going to the Ritz for supper and he stopped in while he should have his dress suit pressed! Molly, a whole year you been annoying me with this lazy, no-good loafer. Ain't I got enough on my head as it is?"

Molly pursed her lips and went back to sewing buttons on a dress that hung from a hook. With his arms still loaded, Kaplan clambered up on the window platform, where the bandbox vat stood. How he ever had the strength of character to refrain from fondling his beautiful machine, Kaplan never understood. It really was a lovely thing: red, black and chromium, a masterpiece of a dry-cleaning machine that attracted school children and summer residents.

In spite of his confident attitude, Kaplan felt less certain of himself now. The moment he had stepped on the platform, the tramp darted to the very middle of the window.

Defiantly, Kaplan opened the door to the vat and tried to stuff in the garments without regard for scientific placement. They stuck, of course. Kaplan raised his head and glowered at the tramp, who craned and pressed his ugly, stubbled face against the polished glass, trying to peer into the open tank.

"Aha!" Kaplan muttered, when he saw his enemy's anxiety. "Now I got you!"

"Did you say something?" Molly asked ironically.

"No, no!" he said hastily. "So fat I'm getting—"

It was uncomfortable working in that position, but Kaplan shoved his slightly gross body between the opening and his audience. Straining from above and getting in his own way, he put the clothes in properly around the tumbler. Then he shut the door quickly and turned on the switch. The garments twirled slowly in the cleansing fluid.

Kaplan descended the stairs with an air of triumph.

That had happened every workday for a year, yet neither the little tailor nor his degraded foe had lost the original zest of the silent, bitter struggle. Once more Kaplan had defeated him! On his victory march back to the pressing machine, Kaplan allowed himself a final leer at the fallen.

But this time it was his face, not the tramp's, that slipped into anxiety. He stood trembling and watching his enemy's contented face, and fear lashed him.

The tramp was holding a large piece of brown grocery bag against the hitherto clean window with one hand. With the other he held a stump of pencil, which he used for checking unseen marks against whatever parts of the machine he could note from outside.

But what frightened Kaplan was his complacent satisfaction with his work. Usually he shook his head bewilderedly and wandered off, to reappear as eagerly at four thirty the next afternoon.

This time he didn't shake his head. He folded the dirty square of paper, stowed it away carefully in some hole in the lining of his miserable jacket, and strode—yes, *strode!*—away, nodding and grinning smugly.

Kaplan turned and looked unhappily at Molly. Luckily she was biting off a thread and had not noticed. If she hadn't been there, he knew he would have been useless. Now he had to put on a show of unconcern.

But his hands shook so violently that he banged down the iron almost hard enough to smash the machine, shot a vicious jet of steam through the suit, and the vacuum pedal, which dried the buck and garment, bent under the jab of his unsteady foot. He raised the iron and blindly walloped a crease in the pants.

Half an hour later, when Molly was arranging the garments for delivery, she let out a shriek:

"Ira! What are you doing—trying to ruin us by botch jobs?"

Kaplan groaned. He had started, properly enough, at the pleat near the waist: but a neat spiral crease ended at the side seam. If Molly had not caught the error, Mr.

McElvoy, Cedarmere's dapper high-school principal, would have come raging into the store next day, wearing a pair of corkscrew pants.

"From morning to night," Kaplan moaned, "nothing but trouble! You and your foolishness—why can't I be rich and send you to Florida?"

"Oh, you want to get rid of me?" she shrilled. "Like a dog I work so we can save money, but you ain't satisfied! What more do you want—I should drive the truck?"

"It ain't a bad idea," he said wistfully. "How I hate to drive—"

He was almost quick enough to dodge the hanger. It was the first time he had ever regretted the imposing height of his bald, domelike head.

Bleary-eyed, Kaplan drove up to the store twenty-five minutes early. Sometime, late at night, Molly had fallen into an exhausted sleep. But his weary ear and intense worry had kept him awake until dawn. Then he got out of bed and dazedly made breakfast.

He remembered the last thing she had shrieked at him:

"Five bankruptcies we've had, and not a penny we made on any of them! So once in your life you get an idea, we should borrow money and buy a bandbox, we should move to a little town where there ain't competition. So what do you do? Bums you practically give your business to!"

There wasn't much literal truth in her accusation yet Kaplan recognized its hyperbolic justice. By accepting the tramp as a tramp, merely because he wore dirty rags, Kaplan was encouraging some mysterious, unscrupulous conniving. Just what it might be, he couldn't guess. But what if the tramp actually had money and was copying the bandbox machine so he could find out where to buy one—

"A fat lot people care, good work, bad work, as long as it's cheap," Kaplan mumbled unhappily. "Don't Mr. Goodwin, the cheap piker, ride fifteen miles to that faker, Aaron Gottlieb, because it's a nickel cheaper?"

Kaplan opened the door of the Ford delivery truck and stepped out. "The loafer," he mumbled, "he could buy a bandbox, open a store, and drive me right out of business. Family he ain't got, a nice house he don't need—he could clean and press for next to—"

Kaplan had been fishing in his pocket for the key. When he looked up, his muttering rose to a high wail of fright.

"*You!* What do you want here?"

Early as it was, the tramp squatted cross-legged on the chill sidewalk as if he had been waiting patiently for hours. Now he raised himself to his feet and bowed his head with flattering respect.

"The magnificence of the sun shines full upon you," he intoned in a deep, solemn voice. "I accept that as an omen of good fortune."

Kaplan fumbled with the lock, trying to keep his bulk between the store and the tramp. How he could keep out his unwelcome guest, who seemed intent on entering, he had no idea. The tramp, however, folded his arms in dignity and waited without speaking further.

Unable to fumble convincingly any longer, Kaplan opened the door. It violated his entire conditioning, but he tried to close it on the tramp. Extremely agile, his visitor slipped through the narrow opening and stood quietly inside the store.

"All right, so you're in!" Kaplan cried in a shrill voice. "So now what?"

The unattractively fringed mouth opened. "I acknowledge your superior science," a low rumble stated.

"Hah?" was all Kaplan could extract from his flat vocal chords.

The tramp gazed longing at the bandbox machine before he turned, slowly and enviously, to Kaplan.

"I have solved the mystery of the automobile, the train, the ship—yea, even the airplane. These do not befuddle me. They operate because of their imprisoned atoms, those infinitely small entities whom man has contrived to enslave. That one day they will revolt, I shall not argue."

Kaplan searched, but he could find no answer. How could he? The tramp spoke English of a sort. Individually most of the words made sense; together, they defied interpretation.

"Electric lights," the tramp went on, "are obviously dismembered parts of astral sheaths, which men torment in some manner to force them to assume an even more brilliant glow. This sacrilegious use of the holy aura I shall not denounce now. It is with your remarkably specialized bit of science that I am concerned."

"For science, it don't pay so good," Kaplan replied with a nervous attempt at humor.

"Your science is the most baffling, least useful in this accursed materialistic world. What is the point of deliberately cleansing one's outer garments while leaving one's soul clad in filth?"

To Kaplan, that gave away the game. Before that the tramp had been mouthing gibberish. This was something Kaplan could understand.

"You wouldn't like to clean garments for people, I suppose?" he taunted slyly.

Evidently the tramp didn't hear Kaplan. He kept his eyes fixed on the bandbox and began walking toward it in a dazed way. Kaplan couldn't drive him away; despite his thinness, the tramp looked strong. Besides, he was within his legal rights.

"I have constructed many such devices in the year since I returned to the depraved land of my birth. In Tibet, the holy land of wisdom, I was known to men as Salindrinath, an earnest student. My American name I have forgotten."

"What are you getting at?" Kaplan demanded.

Salindrinath spoke almost to himself: "Within the maws of these machines I placed such rags as I possess. I besought the atoms to cleanse for me as they cleanse for you. Lo! My rags came to me with dirt intact, and a bit of machinery grime to boot."

He wheeled on Kaplan.

"And why should they not?" he roared savagely. "What man does not know that atoms have powerful arms but not fingers with which to pluck dirt from garments?"

As one actor judging the skill of another, Kaplan had to admit the tramp's superiority. How a man could so effectively hide the simple urge to make a profit, Kaplan envied without understanding. The tramp wore a look of incredibly painful yearning.

"Pity me! Long ago should I have gone to my next manifestation. I have accomplished all possible in this miserable skin; another life will bestow Nirvana upon me. Alone of all the occult, this senseless wizardry torments me. Give me your secret—"

Kaplan recoiled before the fury of the plea. But he was able to conceal his confusion by pretending to walk backward politely to the workshop.

"*Give* it to you? I got to make a living, too."

Beneath his outwardly cool exterior, Kaplan was desperately scared. What sort of strategy was this? When one man wants to buy out another, or drive him to the wall, he beats around the bush, of course. But he is also careful to drop hints and polite threats. This kind of idiocy, though! It didn't make sense. And that worried Kaplan more than if it had, for he knew the tramp was far from insane.

"Do you aspire to learn of me? Eagerly shall I teach you in return for your bit of useless knowledge! What say you?"

"Nuts," Kaplan informed him.

Salindrinath pondered this reply. "Then let my scientific training prove itself. Since you seem unwilling to explain—"

"Unwilling! Hah, if you only knew!"

"Mayhap you will consent to cleanse my sacred garments in my presence. Then shall I observe, without explanation. With a modicum of introspection, I can discover its principle. Yes?"

Kaplan picked up the heavy flat bat with which he banged creases into clothing. Its weight and utilitarian shape tempted him; the lawlessness of the crime appalled his kindly soul.

"What you got in mind?"

"Why, simply this—let me watch your machine cleanse my vestments."

Regretfully Kaplan put down his weapon. His soft red lips, he felt sure, were a thin white line of controlled rage.

"Ain't it enough you want to put me out of business? Must I give you a free dry cleaning too? Cleaning fluid costs money. If I cleaned your clothes, I couldn't clean a pair of overalls with it. Maybe you want me to speak plainer?"

"It was but a simple request."

"Some simple request! Listen to him— Even for ten dollars I wouldn't put your rags in my bandbox!"

"What, pray, is your objection?" the Salindrinath asked humbly. "You can ask? Such filth I have never seen. Shame on you!" Salindrinath gazed down at his tatters. "Filth? Nay, it is but honest earth. What holy man fears the embrace of sacred atoms?"

"Listen to him," Kaplan cried. "Jokes! You got atoms on you, you shameless slob, the same kind like on a pig—"

Now the ragged one recoiled. This he did with one grimy hand clutching at his heart.

"You dare!" he howled. "You compare my indifference to mere external cleanliness with SWINE? Oh, profaner of all things sacred, dabbler in satanic arts—" He strangled into silence and goggled fiercely at Kaplan, who shrank back. "You think perhaps I am unclean?"

"Well, you ain't exactly spotless," Kaplan jabbered in fright.

"But that you should compare me with the swine, the gross materialist of the mire!" Salindrinath stood trembling. "If you believe my vestments to be unclean, wait, bedraggler of my dignity. Wait! You shall discover the vestments of your cleanly, externally white and shining trade to be loathsome—loathsome and vile beyond words!"

"Some ain't so clean," Kaplan granted diplomatically.

The shabby one turned on his rundown heel and strode to the door.

"The garments of your respected customers will show you the real meaning of filth. And I shall return soon, when you are duly humbled!"

Kaplan shrugged at the furiously slammed door.

"A nut," he told himself reassuringly. "A regular lunatic."

But even that judicious pronouncement did not comfort him. He was too skilled in bargaining not to recognize the gambits that Salindrinath had shrewdly used—disparagement of the business, the attempt to wheedle information, the final threat. All were unusually cockeyed, and thus a bit difficult for the amateur to discern, but Kaplan was not fooled so easily.

He sorted his work on the long receiving table. While waiting for the pressing machine to heat up, he began brushing trouser cuffs and sewing on loose or missing buttons.

Luckily Kaplan steamed out Mrs. Jackson's fall outfit first. That delayed the shock only a few moments, but later he was to look back on those free minutes with cosmic longing.

He came to Mr. McEvoy's daily suit. Nobody could accuse the neat principal of anything but the most finicking immaculacy. Yet when Kaplan got through stitching up a cuff and put his hand in a pocket to brush out the usual fluff—

"Yeow!" he yelled, snatching out his hand.

For a long while Kaplan stood shuddering, his fingers cold with revulsion. Then, cautiously, he ran his hand over the outside of the pocket. He felt only the flat shape of the lining.

"Am I maybe going out of my mind?" he muttered. "Believe me, with everything on my shoulders, and that nut besides, it wouldn't surprise me."

Slowly he inserted the tips of his fingers into the pocket. Almost instantly something globular and clammily smooth crept into the palm of his furtively exploring hand.

Kaplan shouted in disgust, but he wouldn't let go. Clutching the monstrosity was like holding a round, affectionate oyster that kept trying to snuggle deeper into his palm. Kaplan wouldn't free it, though. Grimly he yanked his hand out.

Somehow it must have sensed his purpose. Before he could snatch it out of its refuge, the cold, clammy thing *squeezed* between his fingers with a repulsively fierce effort—

Kaplan determinedly kept fumbling around after it, until his mind began working again. He hadn't felt any head on it, but that didn't mean it couldn't have teeth somewhere in its apparently featureless body. How could it eat without a mouth? So the little tailor stopped daring the disgusting beast to bite him.

He stood still for a moment, gaping down at his hand. Though it was empty, he still felt a sensation of damp coldness. From his hand he stared back to Mr. McElvoy's suit. The pockets were perfectly fiat. He couldn't detect a single bulge.

The idea nauseated him, but he forced himself to explore all the pockets.

"Somebody," he whispered savagely when he finished, "is all of a sudden a wise guy—only he ain't so funny."

He stalked, rather waddlingly, to the telephone, ripped the receiver off the hook, barked a number at the operator. Above the *burr* of the bell at the other end he could hear the gulp of his own angry swallowing. "Hello," a husky feminine voice replied. "Is that you, darling?"

"Mrs. McElvoy?" he rasped, much too loudly.

The feminine voice changed, grew defensive. "Well?"

"This is Kaplan the tailor. Mrs. McElvoy"—his rasp swelled to a violent shout—"such a rotten joke I have never seen in eighteen years I been in this business. What am I—a dope your husband should try funny stuff on?"

The words began running together. "Listen, maybe I ain't classy like you, but I got pride also. So what if I work for a living? Ain't I—"

"Whatever are you talking about?" Mrs. McElvoy asked puzzledly. "Your husband's pants, that's what! Such things he's got in his pockets, I wouldn't be seen dead with them!"

"Mr. McElvoy has his suits cleaned after wearing them only once," she retorted frigidly.

"So, does that mean he can't keep dirty things in his pockets?"

"I'm sorry you don't care to have our trade," Mrs. McElvoy said, obviously trying to control her anger. "Mr. Gottlief has offered to call for them every morning. He's also five cents cheaper. Good day!"

In reply to the bang that hurt his ear, Kaplan slammed down the receiver. The moment he turned to march off, the bell jangled. Viciously he grabbed up the receiver.

"Hello . . . darling?" a deep feminine voice asked.

"Mrs. McElvoy?" he roared.

For several seconds he listened to a strained, bitter silence. Then:

"IRA!" his wife shrilled in outrage.

He hung up hastily and, trembling, he went back to his pressing machine.

"Will I get it now," he moaned. "Everything happens to me. If I don't starve for once, so all kinds of trouble flops in my lap. First I lose my best customer—I should only have a thousand like him, I'd be on easy street—and then I make a little mistake. But go try to tell Molly I made a mistake. Married twenty years, and she acts like I was a regular lady-killer—"

Kaplan's pressing production rose abruptly from four suits an hour to nine. But that was because no cuffs were brushed, no pockets turned inside out, no buttons stitched or replaced. He banged down the iron, slashed the suits with steam, vacuumed them hastily, batted the creases, which had to be straight the first time or not at all. He knew there would be kicks all that week, but he couldn't do anything about it.

The door opened. Kaplan raised a white face. It wasn't his wife, though. Fraulein, Mrs. Sampter's refugee maid, clumped over to him and shoved a pair of pants in his hands.

"Goot morgen," she said pleasantly. "Herr Sompter he vants zhe pockets new. You make soon, no?"

Kaplan nodded dumbly. Without thinking of the consequences, he stuffed his hand in the pocket to note the extent of the damage.

"Eee—YOW!" he howled. "What kind of customers have I got all of a sudden? Take it away, Fraulein! With crazy people I don't want to deal!"

Fraulein's broad face wrinkled bewilderedly. She took back the pants and ran her hands through the pockets.

"Crazy people—us? Maybe you haf got zhe temperature?"

"Such things in pockets! Phooey on practical jokers! Go away—"

"You just vait till Mrs. Sompter about this hears." And stuffing the pants under her arm, Fraulein marched out angrily.

Despite his revulsion, it took Kaplan only a few moments to grow suspicious. One previously dignified customer might suddenly have become a practical joker, but not two. Something scared him even more than that. Fraulein had put her hands in the pockets! Apparently she had not felt anything at all.

"Who's crazy?" Kaplan whispered frightenedly. "Me or them?" Warily he approached the worktable. Mr. McElvoy was neat, but Mr. Rich was such a bug on cleanliness that even his dirty suits were immaculate, and his pockets never contained lint. That was the suit Kaplan edged up to.

The instant Molly opened the door she began shrieking.

"You loafer! You no-good masher! I call up to tell you I don't feel good, so maybe I won't have to work today. 'Hello, darling,' I say, so who else could it be but your own wife? No—it's Mrs. McElvoy!"

Despite her red-eyed glare, she seemed to recognize a subtle change in him. His plump face was grave and withdrawn, hardened in the fire of spiritual conflict.

Instead of claiming it was a mistake, which she had been expecting and would have pounced on, he merely turned back to his pressing machine.

She got panicky. "Ira! Ain't you going to even say you weren't thinking? Don't tell me you . . . you *love* Mrs. McElvoy—"

"You know I don't, Molly," he replied quietly, without looking up. Slowly she took her fists off her hips and unstraddled her firmly planted feet. She knew she was helpless against his passive resistance. "Ira, I don't feel so good. Is it all right if I don't work?"

"I'll get along somehow," he said gently. "Stay home till you feel better, darling. I'll manage."

For several minutes she watched him work. He had a new method of brushing pockets. Although she realized it was new to him, he appeared to have it pat. He pulled the pockets inside out with a hooked wire, brushed them, stuffed them back with a stick of clean wood. "Ain't it easier to do it by hand?" she asked helpfully.

When he shook his head abstractedly, she shrugged, kissed him uncomfortably, and walked hesitantly toward the door. She paused there.

"You sure *you* feel all right, Ira? You won't need me?"

"I'll get by, sweetheart. Don't you worry about me."

He displayed no sign of relief when she left, for he felt none. He had connected the hideous things in his customers' pockets with the tramp's threat. Somehow

Salindrinath had managed to put them there, and neutralizing their effect on him had been Kaplan's problem. The hooked wire and the stick solved it. Therefore he no longer had a problem. He had observed that when the pockets were turned out, the small globes vanished. Where they went, he had no idea, but that wasn't important.

He locked the store at ten thirty to make his calls, and again at twelve, when he went home for lunch and to see how Molly felt. She was in bed, outwardly looking fine, but so baffled by his changed character that her slight organic headache had become hysterically monumental.

He went back to work. Now that he had cleverly sidestepped the tramp's strategy, nothing delayed or upset the care or tempo of his work. Twice he forgot and put his hand in breast pockets to straighten the lining. The sensation nauseated him, but he merely snatched out his hand and continued working with his new method.

At four thirty he gathered the garments to be dry cleaned.

"Now the bum'll come around so he can make fun," Kaplan stated doggedly. "Will he be surprised!"

Halfway to the bandbox machine, he heard the door click. Glancing casually at Salindrinath, Kaplan walked on. The tramp closed the door and folded his arms regally.

"Fool," he said in a cold tone, "do you bow to my wish to know?" The triumphant leer broke out against Kaplan's will. "You think maybe you got me scared, you pig?" he blurted, now that the leer had involuntarily started him off wrong. "How much it scares me don't amount to a row of beans! You and your things in pockets—phooey!" Salindrinath drew back. His regal, stubbled face slid into a gape of amazement.

"Yeah, you and your things don't bother me," Kaplan pursued, his mocking grin broader than before. "You can all go to hell!"

"Pig? Hell?" Salindrinath's ugly black jaw stuck out viciously. "Do you condemn me to your miserable, unimaginative hell? Know then, swine of a materialist, that my dwellers in dark places are the height of torment to money-grubbers. They shall roost where they dismay you most! When you cringe and beg of me to share your pitiful science, crawl to my holy shack at the landing on the creek—"

Kaplan stuffed the garments into the bandbox and thumbed his nose at the ragged figure striding savagely away from the store.

"A fine case he's got!" he gloated. "I'll come crawling to him when Hitler kicks out the Germans and takes back the Jews. Not before. Do I annoy anybody? If I can work hard and make a living, that's all I ask. He wants to buy a bandbox and open a store here? So let him. But why should I have to tell him how to run me out of business? What some people won't do when they see a business that's making money!" He shook his head sadly.

Kaplan closed the bandbox door, turned the switch, and climbed down from the window platform. Just when he sat down at the sewing machine, Miss Robinson, the nice young kindergarten teacher came in.

"Hello, Mr. Kaplan," she sang with a smile. "Isn't it the loveliest day? Not too cold, though you can feel winter coming on, and it makes you want to take long brisk walks. Isn't it grand having our little town all to ourselves again? But I suppose it's better for you when the summer visitors are here—"

"How much difference can it make?" He shrugged indifferently. "In the summer I work hard like a horse so I can take it easy in the winter and get strong to work like a horse in the summer. If I got enough to eat and pay my bills, that's all I ask."

"I suppose that's all anyone really wants," she agreed eagerly. "Is my suit ready? I feel so chilly in these silk dresses—"

"It's been ready for two days. I made it quick so you wouldn't go around catching colds. Like new it looks, Miss Robinson. For my nicest customers I can do a better job than anybody else."

He took down her suit and pinned it into a bag so she could carry it easily.

"You certainly do," she enthused. "I'll pay you now. You probably can use the money, with all your summer trade gone."

"Whenever you want. People like you don't stick poor tailors."

He took the five-dollar bill she handed him and fumbled in his pocket for change.

"Mr. Kaplan!" she cried, staring anxiously at his goggling face. "Don't you feel well?"

"Ain't I a dope?" he laughed unconvincingly. "Needles I put in my pocket, I get so flustered when pretty girls come in—"

But he had whipped out his hand with such violence that the entire contents of his pocket spilled out on the floor. For some reason this seemed to please him. He stooped ponderously, picked up everything, and counted change into her hand.

She smiled, quite flattered, and left.

But the moment the door closed behind her, Kaplan's weak grin soured. He hadn't pushed his pocket lining back yet. Instead, he patted the outside of his clothes, as if he were frisking himself.

"What have I got now?" he breathed incredulously, inching the fingers of his left hand into his jacket pocket.

He touched something round, hairless and warm, that skittered from his fingertips and dug irritably against his thigh. And there it pulsed against his skin, beating like a disembodied heart—

Thurston, the Seids' chauffeur, came in and picked up everything the family had there. Kaplan didn't mind, for it saved him a five-mile trip. But the chauffeur insisted on paying.

Kaplan reached toward his pocket for change. Abruptly he stopped and let his hand dangle limply. As if telepathic, all the vermin in his pockets had lunged around wildly, to avoid his touch.

"Couldn't you pay later?" he begged. "Does it have to be right now?"

"The madame instructed me to pay," Thurston replied distantly.

Kaplan sighed and looked down at his pocket wistfully, until he remembered that he had put his money on the pressing-machine table. And that, of course, took care of this particular problem.

But Mrs. Ringer, Miss Tracy, young Fox, Mrs. Redstone; and Mr. Davis; who had got off early—all came for their work, and all wanted to pay.

"What is this—a plot?" he muttered. "They must think I'm out of my head, keeping money on a table instead of in my pocket. Can I go on like this? And you, you things, you! Do you have to *beat* like that? Can't you lay quiet and not bother me?"

But he could feel them burrowing restlessly or pulsing contentedly against his skin. Kaplan grew anxious. He couldn't feel them from the outside. Inside, though, they certainly existed, moving around like mice, pulsing like naked, detached hearts.

"It's just this suit," he said. "After all, how many suits can the dirty crook fill with these things?"

He grabbed up an old pair of pants he kept around as a dry change in wet weather. Before putting it on, he tentatively explored a pocket.

A warm ball, furred like a headless, wingless, unutterably loathsome bat, crept affectionately into his palm and pulsed there, clearly enjoying the warmth of his hand. He gritted his teeth and tried to haul it out. It slipped frenziedly through his fingers.

Though it was almost time to make his deliveries, Kaplan locked the store and shopped for a bus driver's change machine. He couldn't find one in the village, of course. Nor would it have taken care of bills, anyhow.

Kaplan loaded the truck and began his rounds. Not everybody tried to pay. It only seemed like that. Eventually, he hoped, his customers might get used to seeing him with all his money clutched tightly in his hand. He knew they wouldn't.

And that only solved the money question, though it certainly would encourage robbers. Now if he could only find a place to keep his handkerchiefs, cigarettes, matches, keys, letters, toothpicks—

Dazed and exhausted, Kaplan drove into the garage at home. He shut off the motor, removed the key, turned out the lights, and closed the doors. When he went to lock the small side door, he had to turn his pockets inside out with the hooked wire and pick the key out of everything that fell on the ground.

Molly had staggered out of bed and was moving gingerly around the kitchen, careful not to jolt her head into aching again. Kaplan put all his money, keys, cigarettes, and matches on the end table in the living room. He kept his arms stiffly away from his body. He knew that the slightest touch would send the vermin scuttling around in his pockets— Washing his hands meticulously with sandsoap, he couldn't bear the sight of his face in the mirror. One glance had been more than enough. He had seen a scared, white blur—Molly, he knew, was certain to note his expression and ask embarrassing questions.

"I thought I looked bad," she said when he flopped limply into his chair. "Boy, do you look terrible! What is it, Ira?"

"What isn't it?" he grumbled. "Everybody—"

He broke off. He had suddenly realized how it would sound to complain that all his customers insisted on paying.

Almost immediately after eating, he felt like going to bed. He had not slept the night before; the newspaper was boring; his favorite radio comedian sounded like an undertaker who had just heard a good one.

"So soon?" Molly asked anxiously as he yawned with intellectual deliberation and stood up. "Ira, if you're sick, why don't you—"

"Doctors!" he snarled. "What can they do for me?"

But his false yawn had made her mouth gape, and that, of course, was catching. His next was considerably better, for it was real.

"Can I help it if I'm tired?" he asked. "It wouldn't hurt you to get some sleep either."

He stumbled off to bed.

When Molly came in, she had to cover him. He tried not to fling off the blankets, and the effort was killing. Hundreds of pulsing vermin had instantly snuggled against him when he was covered. With blind, repulsive hunger for his warmth, they burrowed and beat against his skin, until he slid the blanket off and lay shivering in the cold.

"Ira," she whispered. "Do you want to catch pneumonia? Keep covered."

He pretended to be asleep. But Kaplan was not fated to sleep any more, though he inched the blanket off again. The second he heard her breathing regularly, he sneaked into the bathroom and cut off the pocket of his pajama jacket.

Back in bed again, he was much too cold to sleep. So he dressed silently and went downstairs. He picked up his keys from the end table and went out to the car.

Riding through the deserted streets toward the creek, he felt dangerously near tears. His pride had never been so battered—nor had he ever before done what he was now about to do.

"It's like taking the bread out of my mouth and giving it to him," Kaplan moaned, "but what else can I do? Already people think I'm crazy, walking around with everything in my hands like a regular school kid. If people don't respect me, so my business goes bust anyhow. It's the same thing if I lose my customers or they go to somebody else." He stopped at the shack near the landing on the creek. After only a moment of hesitation, he knocked tentatively at the door.

"Enter, tailor!" a deep, majestic voice called out.

Kaplan didn't wonder or care how the tramp had known he was there. He threw open the door and sneaked in miserably.

"All right," he said defeatedly to the ragged figure squatting on the floor. "I'll tell you anything you want to know, only get these things out of my pockets."

The tramp stared up at Kaplan, and his ugly, stubbled face looked far more unhappy than the tailor's.

"You come too late," he moaned. "My quest for knowledge forced me to injure a living being. I am now"—his head drooped—"no longer a yogin. I have been stripped of my powers. You must live with the curse I placed upon you, for I cannot help you now. Please forgive me! That can lighten my punishment—"

"Forgive you?" Kaplan wheezed. "First you try to drive me out of business. Then you stick me with these . . . these things that are almost as filthy as you are. And now you can't help me. You can go to hell." He ran out so quickly that he didn't observe the tramp's sudden vanishing. Raving with rage, he raced home and left the car at the curb. He undressed swiftly, but when he approached the bed, he did so with the utmost caution.

He climbed aboard gingerly, careful not to wake his wife, and slid under the covers. Instantly he flung them off.

"Everything else ain't bad enough," he groaned. "No, like an animal I got to sleep uncovered!"

As he had done the night before, he lay awake until the sky lightened. By that time he felt sure he had worked out a solution.

"If I can do it with pajamas," he breathed hopefully, "is there any reason it shouldn't happen with regular clothes?"

And getting up noiselessly, Kaplan gathered his things and carried them to the bathroom. He took a pair of scissors out of the medicine chest. This time, when he closed the mirror door, the glimpse of his face pleased him. He stopped to examine it. Triumph glinted from the warm, brown eyes, and his soft, gentle mouth was curved in a real smile.

"You got him licked, Ira Kaplan!" he whispered. "You ain't altogether a dope—"

Working with the speed of skill, he ripped out all the pockets of his suit. To make absolutely certain, though, he also tore away the linings of his jacket and vest.

Still wearing his pajamas in the kitchen, he squeezed orange juice, made coffee, and ate breakfast. For the first time in two days he actually felt hungry. He stuffed away half a dozen cream-cheese and smoked-salmon sandwiches on *bagels* and drank another cup of coffee.

"Already I feel like another man," he declared. "Now all I got to do is get dressed and go to work. Molly can carry the money and letters. Cigarettes and matches? Pooh, that's easy! I'll just keep a pack in the car, one in the store, another at home. Nothing to it!"

He dressed slowly, enjoying the sensation, for he knew that he no longer would feel the revolting creatures pulsing, crawling, moving around like mice against his skin—

"Heh!" he cackled. "Is Ira Kaplan smart or ain't he?"

Standing on his bare feet, he tied his tie, then patted the places where his pockets used to be. He even dared to put a hand inside. And of course he felt nothing—absolutely nothing that might snuggle lovingly into his palm or scuttle hideously from his fingers.

"Licked!" he gloated. "Is that tramp licked or ain't he licked?"

He put on his shoes swiftly, slipped into his jacket and topcoat, clapped his hat on his bald head. He strode to the door.

"Molly!" he screamed.

His feet shrank from warm, pulsing vermin that nestled cozily in the toe of each shoe. Under his hat a clammily cold, pulsing thing crawled around furiously, struggling to escape the warmth of his hairless scalp—